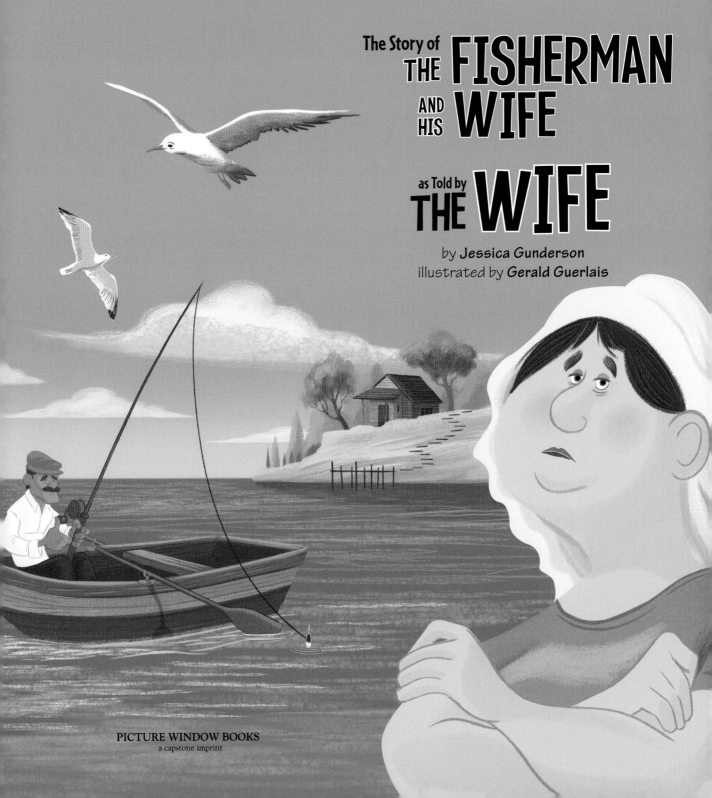

Truthfully, SOMETHING SMELLED FISHY!

The Story of THE FISHERMAN AND HIS WIFE as Told by THE WIFE

by Jessica Gunderson

illustrated by Gerald Guerlais

PICTURE WINDOW BOOKS
a capstone imprint

Editor: Jill Kalz
Designer: Lori Bye
Premedia Specialist: Tori Abraham
The illustrations in this book were created digitally.

⊶⊷❀⊶⊷

Picture Window Books
1710 Roe Crest Drive
North Mankato, MN 56003
www.mycapstone.com

Library of Congress Cataloging-in-Publication Data
Names: Gunderson, Jessica, author. | Guerlais, Gerald, illustrator.
Title: Truthfully, something smelled fishy! : the story of
the fisherman and his wife as told by the wife / by Jessica Gunderson ;
illustrated by Gerald Guerlais.
Description: North Mankato, Minnesota : Picture Window Books, a Capstone
imprint, [2018] | Series: The other side of the story | Summary: A humorous
retelling of the fairy tale, told from the point of view of the fisherman's wife,
who dreams of having plenty of food (she did not have enough to eat as a
child), and is very puzzled about how her poor fisherman husband suddenly
seems able to provide her with everything she ever dreamed of. |
Identifiers: LCCN 2017039804 (print) | LCCN 2017042744 (eBook) |
ISBN 9781515823025 (eBook PDF) | ISBN 9781515822981 (library binding) |
ISBN 9781515823186 (paperback)
Subjects: LCSH: Fairy tales—Adaptations. | Magic—Juvenile fiction. |
Fishers—Juvenile fiction. | Wives—Juvenile fiction. | CYAC: Fairy tales. |
Magic—Fiction. | Greed—Fiction. | Humorous stories. |
LCGFT: Humorous fiction.
Classification: LCC PZ8.G955 (eBook) | LCC PZ8.G955 Tr 2018 (print) |
DDC [E]—dc23
LC record available at https://lccn.loc.gov/2017039804

Printed and bound in the United States of America.
010847S18

I know what you're thinking: *Oh, that fisherman's wife, Isabel . . .*
She was so greedy. And thankless!

Really, though, I was just clueless. It's true! I was also very hungry.

Please, help yourself to some seaweed and let me tell you *my* side
of the story.

When I was growing up, my family didn't have much. We lived in a tiny shack and had little to eat.

I always imagined grand things for my life: castles, fancy clothes, and jewels. But when I married, I married a fisherman. He was a great guy, but he was poor too. I moved from one tiny shack to another.

At least we had plenty of fresh fish to eat, right? Wrong. My husband had to sell everything he caught. We ate a lot of seaweed salad. Gross.

Every night I dreamed of indoor swimming pools and fluffy feather pillows . . . and sizzling steaks with cookie-dough ice cream for dessert. Every morning I woke up in tears.

"Oh, how I wish we lived in a huge house with a big, food-filled kitchen," I told my husband.

"Would that make you happy?" he asked.

"Yes!" I said. "But I know it will never be."

Guess what? The next morning I woke up in a huge house with a big kitchen. And the kitchen was filled with food.

"Thank you, husband, for building me this house!" I cried.

"Well, I . . . ," he started. "I found a flound —"

"No, no," I said before he could finish, "don't say another word. It's just perfect!"

9

At first I was happy. But it didn't last. I remembered my childhood dreams of castles and pretty gowns, and I started to feel sad again.

"Oh, how I wish we lived in a castle," I told my husband. "We'd wear the finest clothes every day. And think of the treats we'd have to eat! Bacon-wrapped shrimp and strawberry pudding, roast turkey and mountains of mashed potatoes . . ."

"Would that make you happy?" he asked.

"Yes!" I said. "But I know it will never be."

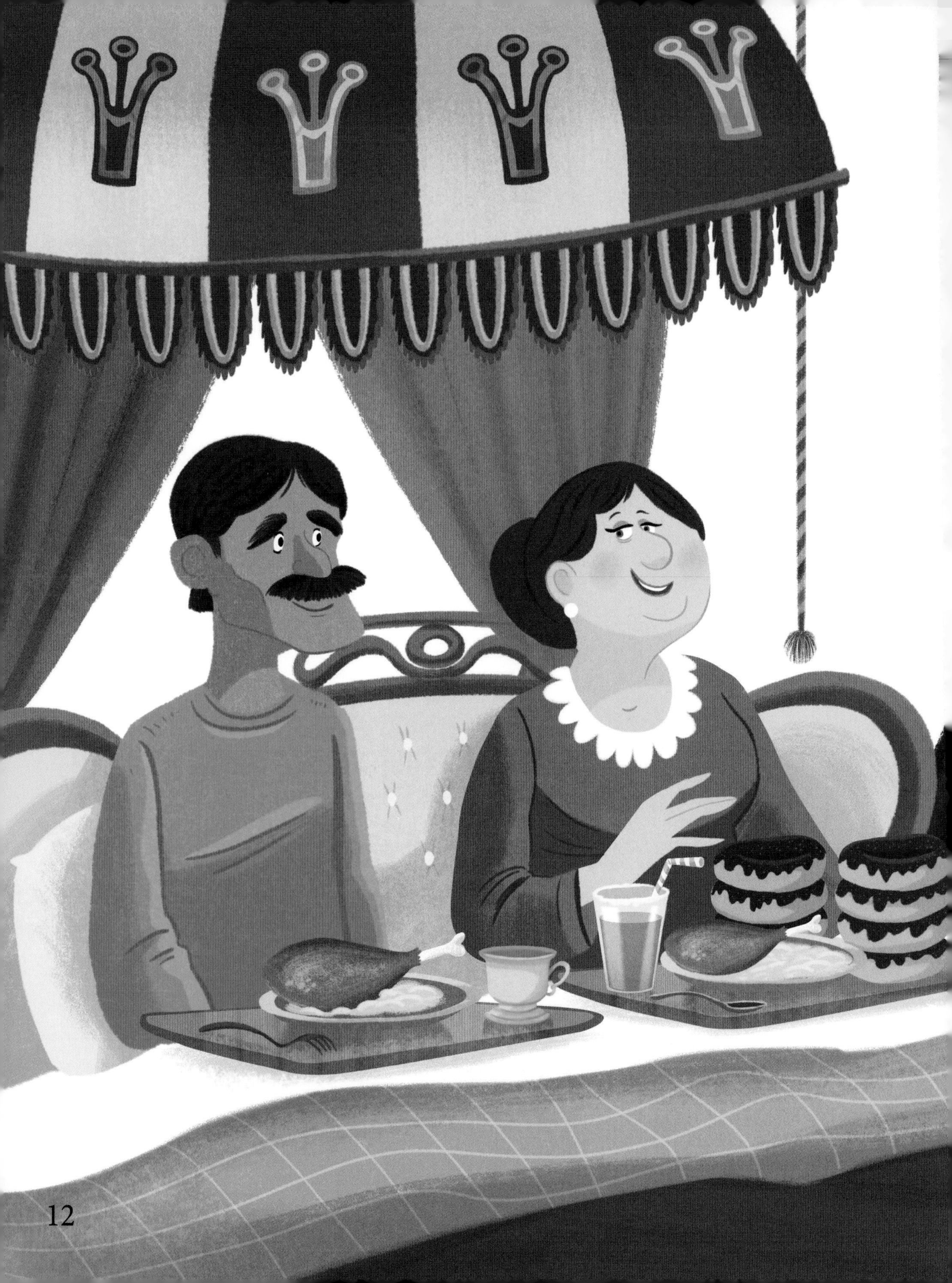

The next morning I woke up to breakfast in bed. Scrambled eggs, chicken, and two stacks of raspberry donuts!

"At your service, Lady Isabel," a maid said.

I couldn't believe my eyes. How could this be? My husband couldn't have built a castle overnight, could he? He must've had help. A LOT of help.

"Thank you for building me this castle!" I told my husband.

"But, it wasn't . . . ," he started. "You see, the flound —"

"Hush now," I said before he could finish. "Eat your drumstick before it gets cold."

13

I should've been very happy — I was living in a castle! But for some reason, I still felt sad, like I was missing something.

"This castle is great," I said to my husband. "But the queen's palace is better, don't you think? Oh, how I wish I were queen! I'd have everything I ever wanted or needed."

"Would that make you happy?" he asked.

"Yes!" I said. "But I know it will never be."

The next morning I couldn't raise my head. Something very heavy sat upon it. A crown!

"Good morning, Queen Isabel," a group of servants said.

I had become queen overnight. Me! My palace had an indoor water park, a movie theater, and a zoo filled with animals from around the world. It had a go-cart track and mini-golf course. It even had its own pizza and ice-cream shop!

How did all of this happen? Was my husband stealing money? Was he a magician or wizard? Was I under a spell?

Something fishy was going on.

"Thank you for making me queen," I told my husband.

"But I didn't . . . ," he started. "The flound —"

"I don't know how you're doing it," I said before he could finish. "But I'd like one more thing. I'd like to be able to make the sun rise and set whenever I want."

"And then you'd be happy?" he asked.

"Yes!" I said. "For sure!"

That night, I secretly followed my husband to the beach. How could he ever grant my latest wish? I hid behind a rock and watched.

He shouted something at the sea, and a giant fish rose from the water. It was magnificent! We could feast on that beast for days!

I burst from my hiding spot and scooped up the fish in my husband's net.

"No! Don't!" my husband cried.

But I didn't listen. I carried the fish back to the palace and had my chef fry it up for dinner.

As soon as the fish hit the frying pan, my crown disappeared. So did the servants and the palace. My husband and I were back in our tiny shack.

"I *told* you not to cook the fish!" my husband said with a sigh.

"But I didn't . . . ," I started. "What kind of fish is this, anyway? It's very —"

"*Flounder*," he said before I could finish. "It's a *flounder*, my dear."

Think About It

The fisherman's wife, Isabel, wishes for grander and grander things as the story goes on. Do you think she should've stopped wishing when she got the huge house with the food-filled kitchen? Why or why not?

Look online to find the classic version of "The Fisherman and His Wife." Describe how the character of the fisherman's wife looks and acts. Compare and contrast that wife with the wife in this version of the story.

If the fisherman told this story instead of his wife, what details might he tell differently? What if the fish told the story? How would its point of view differ?

Glossary

character—a person, animal, or creature in a story
point of view—a way of looking at something
version—an account of something from a certain point of view

Read More

Felix, Rebecca. *The Fisherman and His Wife.* Mankato, Minn.: Child's World, 2013.

Grimm, Jacob. *Gris Grimly's Tales from the Brothers Grimm: Being a Selection from the Household Stories Collected by Jacob and Wilhelm Grimm.* New York: Balzer + Bray, 2016.

Stewart, Whitney. *A Catfish Tale: A Bayou Story of the Fisherman and His Wife.* Chicago: Albert Whitman & Company, 2014.

Internet Sites

Use FactHound to find Internet sites related to this book.

Visit *www.facthound.com*

Just type in 9781515822981 and go.

Look for all the books in the series:

Believe Me, Goldilocks Rocks!
Believe Me, I Never Felt a Pea!
For Real, I Paraded in My Underpants!
Frankly, I'd Rather Spin Myself a New Name!
Frankly, I Never Wanted to Kiss Anybody!
Honestly, Our Music Stole the Show!
Honestly, Red Riding Hood Was Rotten!
Listen, My Bridge Is SO Cool!
No Kidding, Mermaids Are a Joke!

No Lie, I Acted Like a Beast!
No Lie, Pigs (and Their Houses) CAN Fly!
Really, Rapunzel Needed a Haircut!
Seriously, Cinderella Is SO Annoying!
Seriously, Snow White Was SO Forgetful!
Truly, We Both Loved Beauty Dearly!
Trust Me, Hansel and Gretel Are SWEET!
Trust Me, Jack's Beanstalk Stinks!
Truthfully, Something Smelled Fishy!

Check out projects, games and lots more at
www.capstonekids.com

24